THE UNSOLVED CASE OF MAPLEWOOD

By

Richard Trillion Mantey

Table of Contents

Dedication

This book is dedicated to every person who has ever searched for answers...

To those who have waited in silence,

who have lived with questions that time could not erase,

and who have carried the weight of the unknown with quiet strength.

It is for the ones who continue to believe—

that truth matters,

that every story deserves to be heard,

and that even in uncertainty... There is resilience.

And above all, it is for those who understand that some journeys are not about closure—

but about the courage to keep seeking.

Acknowledgments

This book is a reflection of many influences, insights, and inspirations.

I would like to express my deep gratitude to those who dedicate their lives to seeking truth—investigators, forensic professionals, legal experts, and researchers whose relentless pursuit of answers continues to inspire stories like this one.

To the readers—thank you for your curiosity, your imagination, and your willingness to step into complex and thought-provoking narratives. Your engagement gives life to every page.

To those who have ever faced uncertainty, unanswered questions, or moments without closure—this story is, in many ways, for you.

And finally, to the creative spirit that drives all storytelling—thank you for reminding us that even in mystery, there is meaning.

Chapter 1: The Day It All Began

The Disappearance

The small town of Maplewood had always been a quiet place, known for its friendly neighbors and picturesque landscapes. However, everything changed on a chilly autumn evening when Thomas Reed, a local librarian, mysteriously vanished without a trace. His disappearance sent shockwaves through the community, stirring whispers of unease and speculation among residents who had always felt safe in their tight-knit environment. The sense of normalcy was shattered, leaving the townsfolk grappling with unanswered questions and a gnawing fear that something sinister lurked beneath the surface.

Detective Clara Hargrove, a seasoned investigator with years of experience, was assigned to the case. She approached the investigation with methodical precision, meticulously piecing together the last known movements of Thomas. Interviews were conducted with family members, friends, and coworkers, each revealing fragments of his life that painted a complicated picture. As Clara sifted through the evidence, she began to uncover inconsistencies in the statements, hinting that not everyone was being entirely truthful about the librarian's character and habits.

Forensic science played a crucial role in the investigation. Clara consulted with experts who analyzed Thomas's belongings, seeking any clues that could lead them closer to understanding his fate. Fingerprints, DNA samples, and digital footprints were examined with care, but the results were often frustratingly inconclusive. Each lead seemed to fizzle out, leaving Clara with more questions than answers and a growing sense of urgency to crack the case before it grew cold.

As weeks turned into months, the investigation took a toll on Clara. The pressure from the community weighed heavily on her shoulders, especially as families began to lose faith in the police's ability to solve such a high-profile disappearance. Yet, Clara remained steadfast, driven by an unyielding determination to bring closure to Thomas's loved ones. She understood that the psychological aspect of the case was just as important as the physical evidence; she needed to delve into the minds of those who knew him, searching for motives that might reveal why someone would want to harm him.

In the end, the disappearance of Thomas Reed became more than just a case; it evolved into a symbol of the secrets that Maplewood harbored. As Detective Hargrove continued to push forward, she uncovered layers of intrigue that suggested the librarian's life was far more complex than anyone had imagined. Each step closer to the truth illuminated not only the darkness surrounding Thomas's fate but also the very fabric of the community itself, forever changed by the unresolved mystery that refused to close, leaving an indelible mark on the hearts of those who remained.

The Initial Investigation

As the sun dipped below the horizon, casting long shadows over Maplewood, the initial investigation into the mysterious disappearance of local resident Sarah Jenkins began. Detective Samuel Hargrove, a seasoned investigator known for his methodical approach, arrived at the scene where Sarah was last seen. The quaint town, with its picturesque streets and tight-knit community, was shaken by the incident, and Hargrove felt the weight of the townsfolk's expectations on his shoulders. He knew that every detail mattered, and the first steps of the investigation would be crucial in unraveling the truth behind Sarah's fate.

Hargrove meticulously examined the area, taking in the surroundings with a detective's keen eye. He noted the placement of the park bench where Sarah was said to have been sitting, the nearby path that wound through the trees, and the fading light that quickly transformed the scene into an eerie twilight. Evidence collection began immediately; he instructed his team to gather any potential clues, from discarded items to footprints in the dirt. Each piece of evidence could lead to a breakthrough, and Hargrove's experience taught him that nothing should be overlooked.

Interviews with Sarah's friends and family were next on Hargrove's agenda. He understood that psychological profiling could offer insights into her state of mind leading up to her disappearance. Each interview was approached with sensitivity, as he sought to build a comprehensive picture of Sarah's life. The conversations revealed layers of her personality—her struggles, relationships, and recent changes that might have contributed to her actions. Hargrove listened intently, knowing that often the smallest detail could unlock the door to understanding the bigger mystery.

The detective also turned to the town's historical records, seeking patterns in unresolved cases that might mirror Sarah's situation. Maplewood held its own secrets, and Hargrove believed that the town's past could hold clues to the present. He engaged with local historians and longtime residents, threading together stories that spanned decades. Hargrove's persistence in exploring these connections was fueled by the hope that they might lead him to a fresh perspective on the case.

As days turned into weeks, the investigation into Sarah's disappearance faced numerous challenges. The lack of concrete evidence and the psychological toll on the community weighed heavily on Hargrove. Yet, he remained determined, fueled by the belief that every unsolved case had its own story waiting to be uncovered. With each passing day, he compiled his findings, piecing together the fragments of Sarah's life, convinced that the truth was still out there, just beyond the shadows of Maplewood.

A Town in Shock

The sun had barely risen over Maplewood when the news broke: a beloved local figure had been found dead under suspicious circumstances. As the townspeople slowly emerged from their homes, the shock was palpable in the cool morning air. Conversations were hushed, and worried glances exchanged as families gathered on their porches, grappling with the reality that their quiet, close-knit community was now the center of a grim investigation. This was not just any tragedy; it was a moment that would forever alter the fabric of their lives, leaving an indelible mark on the town's history.

Detective Sarah Mitchell, a seasoned investigator with years of experience under her belt, arrived at the scene with a heavy heart. She had seen her share of tragedies, but there was something particularly unsettling about this case. The victim, a respected teacher, had touched many lives, and the outpouring of grief was evident. As she began her meticulous examination of the crime scene, she noted every detail: the position of the body, the scattered belongings, and the absence of any signs of forced entry. Each clue held the potential to unlock the mystery, but time was of the essence.

Interviews with the townsfolk revealed a complex web of relationships and hidden secrets. Friends, neighbors, and even former students shared their memories, each providing a piece of a larger puzzle. Detective Mitchell listened carefully, probing for inconsistencies and motives that might have led to such a heinous act. It quickly became clear that Maplewood, while seemingly idyllic, harbored deep-seated rivalries and unspoken tensions. The more she uncovered, the more the town's facade began to crack, revealing shadows lurking beneath its surface.

As days turned into weeks, the investigation stalled, and the town's initial shock transformed into frustration. Maplewood had always prided itself on its unity, but now the unease was palpable. Rumors spread like wildfire, and fingers were pointed in every direction as fear took hold. Detective Mitchell remained steadfast, determined to bring justice to the victim and closure to the community. She understood that the case was more than just a job; it was a lifeline for the town's hope and healing.

In the end, the case of the beloved teacher would not be just another statistic in the annals of unsolved mysteries. It was a testament to the resilience of a community grappling with loss and uncertainty.

As Detective Mitchell pieced together the fragments of evidence, she not only sought justice for the victim but also aimed to restore a sense of safety and trust in Maplewood. The journey was far from over, but with each discovery, she inched closer to unraveling the truth and bringing peace back to a town in shock.

Chapter 2: The Detective's Perspective

Meet Detective Harris

Detective Harris stood at the heart of Maplewood, a small town with secrets buried deeper than its cobblestone streets. Known for his meticulous approach, Harris was a figure often seen in the local diner, sipping black coffee while reviewing case files. His reputation for solving the unsolvable had become the stuff of legend, drawing both admiration and skepticism from his peers. With salt-and-pepper hair and a keen eye for detail, he embodied the archetype of a detective who had seen too much but remained undeterred by the darkness he encountered in his line of work.

For Harris, every unsolved case was an unfinished puzzle, haunting him like a ghost that lingered in the shadows. He believed that each crime held the key to understanding the human psyche, and he approached his investigations with an analytical mind and a compassionate heart. His methodology was straightforward: gather evidence, interview witnesses, and, crucially, listen. Over the years, he had developed an uncanny ability to read people, often discerning truths hidden behind their facades. This skill set him apart in a field where intuition was as vital as forensic evidence.

The case that refused to close was one that had long haunted him, a missing person report that led to a rabbit hole of confusion and despair. The disappearance of a local girl left ripples of fear throughout the community, and despite his best efforts, the trail had gone cold. Harris would often revisit the scene, retracing steps and speaking to anyone who might shed light on the situation. Each time he returned, he felt the weight of responsibility, not just to the victim but to the town that had placed its trust in him.

In his pursuit of justice, Harris often found himself tangled in the complexities of human emotions and relationships. The small-town dynamics presented unique challenges; everyone knew everyone, and secrets were often shielded by a veneer of normalcy. As he navigated through layers of deceit, he relied on his instincts to discern ally from adversary. The psychological profiling of potential suspects became a crucial part of his strategy, allowing him to anticipate their next moves, as if he were playing a high-stakes game of chess.

As the investigation wore on, Harris remained steadfast, fueled by a relentless pursuit of truth. The case, much like the town itself, was a tapestry woven with threads of hope, despair, and resilience. Each new lead was a spark in the darkness, reigniting his determination to bring closure to the families affected by the tragedy. In Maplewood, where every corner seemed to whisper stories of the past, Detective Harris knew that even the coldest cases could eventually thaw, revealing the truths that had long eluded him.

The Evidence Pile

In the heart of Maplewood lies a collection of evidence, gathered meticulously over the years, known informally as "The Evidence Pile." This archive, a mix of tangible artifacts and intangible memories, serves as a testament to the town's unresolved mysteries. Each item tells a story, a fragment of a larger puzzle that has confounded both the locals and the detectives who have come to investigate. The evidence is a constant reminder that some cases refuse to close, lingering in the minds of those who seek the truth.

The first item in the pile is an old, weathered jacket found near the crime scene. It bears the faint scent of cigarette smoke and an unsettling stain that has yet to be identified. Forensic experts have tested it repeatedly, yet the answers remain elusive. The jacket's presence evokes questions about its owner – was he a victim, a suspect, or merely an innocent bystander caught in a tragic circumstance? Each new examination breathes life into the cold case, igniting hope that one day, this piece of fabric might unveil long-hidden secrets.

Interviews with local residents have also contributed to the growing mound of evidence. Many recall the fateful night when the crime occurred, their memories tinged with fear and speculation. Some claim to have seen a shadowy figure lurking near the site, while others insist they heard the unmistakable sound of a struggle. These accounts, although often conflicting, have been documented and re-examined, revealing the complexities of human memory and the intertwining of truth and perception. Each retelling adds layers to the case, emphasizing the importance of persistence in the pursuit of justice.

As the years roll on and technology advances, forensic science plays an increasingly critical role in the investigation. New methods of analysis, such as DNA profiling and digital forensics, have breathed new life into old evidence. Items that once seemed insignificant can now yield crucial information, leading detectives down previously unexplored paths. The Evidence Pile grows not only in physical size but also in potential, as each new technique offers a glimmer of hope for closure in a case that has haunted the town for too long.

Ultimately, The Evidence Pile represents the essence of detective work — a relentless quest for truth amidst uncertainty. It embodies the struggles of those who refuse to give up, who believe that every clue, no matter how small, can lead to a breakthrough. As Maplewood continues to grapple with its mysteries, the evidence remains a symbol of resilience, reminding all who encounter it that the case may be cold, but the pursuit of justice is anything but.

A Case with No Leads

In the small town of Maplewood, the investigation into the disappearance of local resident Claire Thompson had reached an impasse. Months had passed since her last known whereabouts, and despite the tireless efforts of Detective Mark Ellis, the case seemed to grow colder by the day. The community was haunted by whispers of what might have happened, yet no credible leads surfaced to guide the investigation. With every passing week, hope waned, but the determination to uncover the truth remained at the forefront of Ellis's mind.

The absence of physical evidence only compounded the mystery. Every nook and cranny of Maplewood had been meticulously searched; the woods where Claire vanished had yielded nothing but silence. Interviews with family, friends, and acquaintances provided little insight. Each person's recollection seemed to fade like echoes in a canyon, leaving Ellis with a growing sense of frustration. In the world of detective fiction, such scenarios often lead to breakthroughs, but in reality, they often lead to dead ends, where the detective must dig deeper into the psyche of the town and its inhabitants.

As months turned into years, the town began to adjust to the idea of living with an unsolved mystery. Some residents grew resentful, feeling that the police had abandoned their quest. Others turned to conspiracy theories, weaving tales that only served to muddy the waters further. Detective Ellis, however, clung to a methodical approach. He understood that in cold cases, patience is as critical as any forensic evidence. Each piece of information, no matter how trivial, could hold the key to unlocking the truth.

Psychological profiling became a pivotal aspect of Ellis's strategy. He began to analyze the behaviors and statements of those closest to Claire. Understanding the motivations and potential secrets of the townspeople became essential. As he delved deeper into the fabric of Maplewood, he uncovered hidden histories and relationships that had long been buried. This methodical unearthing of the past would prove vital, revealing connections that might not have been apparent initially.

Ultimately, the case of Claire Thompson refused to close, serving as a testament to the complexities of human nature and the quiet desperation that often accompanies unresolved mysteries. Detective Ellis learned that every unsolved case is not just about the evidence left behind, but about the stories of those affected by the absence. In Maplewood, the echoes of Claire's disappearance would continue to resonate, challenging both the detective and the town to confront their past while seeking justice for a future that remained uncertain.

Chapter 3: Cold Cases and Their Impact

The Nature of Cold Cases

The nature of cold cases is both intriguing and frustrating, capturing the attention of seasoned detectives and armchair sleuths alike. These are the mysteries that refuse to fade away, lingering in the shadows of a small town like Maplewood. Each case represents a story left untold, a puzzle demanding resolution. Unlike typical investigations that conclude with a tidy resolution, cold cases often leave more questions than answers, drawing investigators into a labyrinth of unresolved clues and forgotten evidence.

At the heart of a cold case lies the relentless pursuit of truth. Detectives revisit evidence, re-interview witnesses, and apply modern forensic techniques to breathe new life into investigations that have stagnated. The passage of time can bring new insights; advancements in technology often enable the analysis of evidence that was previously deemed insufficient. The age-old adage, "time heals all wounds," holds little weight here; instead, time becomes a double-edged sword, allowing both memories to fade and fresh perspectives to emerge.

Psychological profiling plays a crucial role in understanding the minds of those who commit crimes that remain unsolved. By examining patterns of behavior, motivations, and potential connections between victims and suspects, investigators can develop a clearer picture of what transpired. This methodical approach mirrors the narrative style of classic detective fiction, where the process of deduction and reasoning propels the story forward. For readers who appreciate the nuances of character and motive, the psychological aspect of cold cases adds a compelling layer of depth to an already complex mystery.

The legal troubles that often accompany cold cases present another layer of difficulty. Even when new evidence surfaces, the path to justice can be fraught with obstacles. Legal statutes, jurisdictional issues, and the need for irrefutable proof often complicate the resolution of these cases. Investigators must navigate a web of legalities that can stifle progress, leading to a sense of frustration that resonates with both detectives and readers alike. Understanding these challenges provides insight into why some cases elude resolution for decades.

Ultimately, cold cases encapsulate the essence of mystery and the human experience. They challenge our innate desire for closure while simultaneously inviting curiosity and investigation. For fans of traditional detective fiction, these unresolved stories evoke a sense of nostalgia, drawing parallels to the classic investigations of iconic literary detectives. The ongoing quest for answers in the face of uncertainty reflects a timeless struggle that resonates deeply with readers, making the exploration of cold cases a captivating journey into the unknown.

Community Response

In the small town of Maplewood, the mystery surrounding the unsolved case had a profound impact on the community. Residents, who once lived in harmony, found themselves divided as whispers of suspicion and fear spread. The disappearance of local teenager Emily Parker had turned from a tragic event into a source of speculation, with neighbors questioning one another's motives. The town's serene facade was beginning to crack, revealing the underlying tensions that had been simmering just below the surface.

As the investigation progressed, the community rallied together in unexpected ways. Candlelight vigils were held, and posters of Emily adorned shop windows, showcasing a collective desire for closure. Local businesses donated funds to support the investigation, while volunteers organized search parties, combing the nearby woods in hopes of finding new evidence. This united front highlighted the resilience of Maplewood's residents, who were determined not to let their town become defined by a tragedy.

However, as time passed without answers, frustration grew among the townsfolk. Many felt the police were not doing enough, leading to heated town hall meetings where residents voiced their concerns. A number of them took it upon themselves to conduct their own investigations, fueled by a mix of desperation and determination. This grassroots movement often collided with the official investigation, creating further complications as amateur sleuths followed leads that sometimes led nowhere.

In the midst of this chaos, a local journalist sought to uncover the truth through meticulous research and interviews. His articles not only chronicled the investigation's progress but also captured the emotional toll on the community. He delved into the psychology behind the residents' reactions, exploring how fear and suspicion could erode trust. Through his lens, the story of Maplewood transformed from a mere mystery into a reflection of human nature and the lengths people would go to find answers.

Ultimately, the community's response to the unsolved case of Emily Parker became a testament to their collective strength. Despite the uncertainty that hung over them, they demonstrated an unwavering commitment to justice and healing. The mystery, while unresolved, fostered a sense of unity among the townsfolk, reminding them that even in the face of darkness, hope could be found in shared purpose and resilience. As they continued to seek closure, the spirit of Maplewood remained unbroken, determined to uncover the truth behind the shadows that loomed over their beloved town.

The Weight of Uncertainty

In the small town of Maplewood, uncertainty loomed like a thick fog, shrouding every corner and crevice with an air of mystery. The unsolved case of the missing local artist had become a haunting specter that clung to the community. Every whispered conversation in the coffee shop, every furtive glance in the park, seemed to carry the weight of questions left unanswered. The absence of closure had created a ripple effect, affecting not just the family of the artist, but the very fabric of the town itself.

Detective Sam Harper, a seasoned investigator with a penchant for detail, felt the burden of this uncertainty more than anyone. With each passing year, the case became not just a professional challenge but also a personal obsession. He meticulously reviewed every piece of evidence, every interview conducted, and every lead that had gone cold. The files were thick with details, yet the truth remained elusive, like a shadow slipping away just as it was about to be caught.

As Harper delved deeper into the artist's life, he uncovered layers of complexity that added to the uncertainty. Friends and family members provided conflicting accounts of the artist's last days, their memories tinged with the emotions of loss and guilt. It became evident that the artist had been a figure of intrigue, with secrets that perhaps even those closest to him were unaware of. Each disclosure added weight to the mystery, complicating the path toward resolution.

The psychological toll of the unresolved case began to manifest in the community, turning neighbors into skeptics and friends into adversaries. Rumors swirled, feeding on the uncertainty that had settled over Maplewood. Harper understood that the mind often creates its own narratives, filling the gaps left by the absence of facts. In a town where secrets festered, the stakes were high, and the truth was a fragile commodity, easily overshadowed by fear and speculation.

In the end, the weight of uncertainty would not just define the investigation but also illuminate the essence of human nature itself. It revealed how deeply intertwined lives could become in the face of unresolved questions. As Harper continued his pursuit of the truth, he was reminded that sometimes, the journey is as significant as the destination. The case of the missing artist would not be easy to solve, but it was a testament to the enduring spirit of inquiry, a reminder that some mysteries, no matter how heavy they may feel, are worth the relentless pursuit of answers.

Chapter 4: Forensic Science Unveiled

The Role of Forensics

In the heart of every unsolved case lies the vital role of forensics, a discipline that has revolutionized the way we approach crime-solving. Forensic science encompasses a variety of techniques and methodologies that help detectives piece together the puzzle of a crime scene. From DNA analysis to ballistics, these scientific advancements provide critical evidence that can either confirm or challenge a suspect's narrative. In the case of Maplewood, the lingering mystery hinges on the forensic evidence that has remained untouched for decades, waiting for the right detective to make sense of it all.

Detective work is not merely about intuition and experience; it is deeply rooted in the meticulous collection and analysis of evidence. In Maplewood, the original investigation may have faltered, but modern forensic techniques offer a lifeline. With advancements in technology, cold case units can revisit old evidence, applying new methods that were not available at the time of the initial investigation. This means that every hair, fiber, and trace element collected from the scene has the potential to tell a story, bringing us closer to the truth.

One of the most compelling aspects of forensic science is its ability to engage with psychological profiling. Understanding the criminal mind can significantly aid in narrowing down suspects, especially in a close-knit community like Maplewood. By analyzing patterns of behavior, motives, and past criminal records, forensic psychologists can provide insights that guide detectives in their interviews. This psychological angle adds another layer of complexity to the investigation, merging the hard evidence with the softer science of human behavior.

As new evidence emerges, legal challenges often arise, complicating the pathway to justice. The case of Maplewood illustrates how unresolved mysteries can lead to prolonged legal troubles, especially when forensic evidence is re-examined. Detectives must navigate the delicate balance between uncovering new leads and respecting the legal implications of their findings. This intricate dance between forensics and the law is crucial for ensuring that justice is served, even if it takes years to achieve.

Ultimately, the role of forensics in the Maplewood case underscores the persistence required in cold case investigations. It highlights the importance of not only the evidence itself but also the dedication of those who seek to uncover the truth. For readers who appreciate methodical case-solving and the gradual unveiling of secrets, the journey through forensic science is as captivating as the mystery itself. As detectives delve deeper into the layers of evidence, they remind us that every unsolved case still holds the potential for resolution, waiting for the right moment to be brought back to light.

Techniques That Changed the Game

In the realm of detective fiction, certain techniques have emerged as transformative, altering the very fabric of how mysteries are unraveled. The art of methodical case-solving has gained prominence, where detectives meticulously sift through clues, piecing together the puzzle one fragment at a time. This slow yet steady approach resonates with readers who appreciate the intellectual rigor behind solving a case, echoing classic investigation stories that have captivated audiences for generations.

Interviews have also evolved into a cornerstone of modern detective work. The dynamic between the investigator and the interviewee can unveil hidden truths or obscure motivations. Readers are drawn to the psychological dance that unfolds during these exchanges, often revealing more than just facts; they expose the emotional undercurrents that drive human behavior. This technique adds depth to the narrative, allowing for a richer exploration of character and motive.

Forensic science has revolutionized the investigation landscape, providing tools that were once the stuff of fiction. Advances in DNA analysis, fingerprinting, and digital forensics have enabled detectives to solve cases that might have remained cold for decades. For readers of traditional mystery, this intersection of science and sleuthing introduces a modern twist to the classic whodunit, making the impossible possible and reigniting the pursuit for justice in long-lingering cases.

The psychological profiling of criminals has become an invaluable technique that gives depth to the narrative, helping to paint a vivid picture of the perpetrator's mind. Through understanding the motivations and behaviors of offenders, detectives can narrow down suspects with remarkable accuracy. This method not only enhances the plot but also engages readers who relish the challenge of understanding the complex interplay between psychology and crime.

Lastly, the legal troubles surrounding unsolved cases can add layers of tension and intrigue. The bureaucratic hurdles faced by detectives often mirror the obstacles encountered in real-life investigations. This element resonates with those who appreciate the procedural aspects of detective stories, as it highlights the persistence required to seek justice in a system that can sometimes feel obstructive. The combination of these techniques creates a compelling narrative that keeps readers on the edge of their seats, eager to see how the case will ultimately unfold.

New Advances in Technology

In the realm of mystery and detective fiction, technology has become an indispensable ally for modern investigators. Gone are the days when sleuths relied solely on intuition and physical evidence. Today, forensic science has evolved dramatically, employing advanced techniques such as DNA analysis and digital forensics to unravel cold cases. This technological revolution not only enhances the accuracy of investigations but also opens new avenues for solving mysteries that have lingered for decades.

The integration of artificial intelligence into crime-solving has further transformed the landscape of detective work. AI algorithms can sift through vast amounts of data, identifying patterns and connections that might elude even the most seasoned detectives. For example, psychological profiling powered by AI can help predict criminal behavior, guiding investigators toward possible suspects with remarkable precision. This method of harnessing technology allows for a more strategic approach to investigations, ensuring that no stone is left unturned.

Moreover, the advent of digital communication has changed the way detectives gather evidence and conduct interviews. With the rise of social media, investigators can now trace leads and connect with witnesses more effectively than ever before. Online platforms provide a wealth of information that can be crucial in piecing together the puzzle of an unresolved case. Detectives can monitor digital footprints, gathering insights that would have been impossible to obtain in the past.

In small towns like Maplewood, where secrets often lie buried beneath layers of familiarity, technology serves as a beacon of hope. Local law enforcement agencies are increasingly adopting cutting-edge tools to aid in their investigations. From body cameras to mobile forensic labs, these advancements empower officers to document evidence meticulously and ensure transparency in their methods. The blend of tradition and modernity in investigative practices resonates deeply with audiences who appreciate the methodical unraveling of mysteries.

As the story of "The Case That Refused to Close" unfolds, the advancements in technology become pivotal in solving the lingering enigmas. Readers familiar with classic investigation narratives will find comfort in the familiar tropes, yet they will also be intrigued by how modern tools reshape the narrative. The marriage of traditional detective work with contemporary technology holds the promise of closure, breathing new life into the age-old quest for truth in small-town mysteries.

Chapter 5: The Psychology of Crime

Understanding Criminal Minds

Understanding criminal minds is essential for unraveling the intricacies of unsolved cases like the one in Maplewood. Detectives often find themselves delving not just into the facts of a crime, but also into the psychology of those who commit them. Each criminal leaves behind a unique fingerprint of motives, behaviors, and patterns that can reveal much about their psyche. By understanding the motivations and emotional triggers of a suspect, investigators can better approach the case, ensuring that no stone is left unturned in their pursuit of justice.

Psychological profiling is a tool that has gained prominence in modern detective work. It allows investigators to construct a profile of the perpetrator based on the nature of the crime and the evidence left behind. In the Maplewood case, understanding the criminal's mindset is crucial for generating leads and narrowing down potential suspects. This methodical approach not only aids in solving the current case but also provides insights into similar unresolved cases, creating a framework for future investigations.

The art of interviewing witnesses and suspects is another critical component of understanding criminal minds. Skilled detectives know that each conversation can yield vital clues or reveal inconsistencies in a suspect's story. In small towns like Maplewood, where everyone knows each other, the nuances of human interaction become even more pronounced. Detectives must be adept at reading body language and emotional cues, as these can often indicate whether a person is hiding something or telling the truth.

Persistence is key in cold case investigations. The passage of time can often lead to new evidence or the willingness of witnesses to come forward. In the Maplewood case, the community's lingering unease about unresolved crimes keeps the pressure on law enforcement to revisit old leads. Detectives must remain patient and methodical, exploring every avenue, even those that seem unlikely, as they piece together the puzzle of the past.

Ultimately, understanding criminal minds is not just about solving individual cases; it is about uncovering the secrets that lie within each community. The fear, suspicion, and unresolved questions that linger can have a profound impact on the lives of residents. As detectives continue to probe into the minds of criminals, they also begin to heal the rifts in their communities, bringing closure not only to the case at hand but also to the emotional scars left by unresolved crimes.

Profiling Techniques

Profiling techniques have become an essential tool in modern detective work, allowing investigators to develop a comprehensive understanding of criminal behavior. By analyzing the psychological traits, motivations, and patterns of offenders, detectives can create profiles that guide their investigations. This methodical approach not only aids in narrowing down potential suspects but also assists in predicting future actions of those who may continue to commit crimes. In the context of the Maplewood case, profiling can provide valuable insights into the mind of a perpetrator who has eluded capture for years.

The process of creating a criminal profile is both an art and a science. Investigators gather data from various sources, including crime scene evidence, victimology, and historical patterns of criminal behavior. By synthesizing this information, they can identify common characteristics of offenders, such as their background, psychological makeup, and modus operandi. This systematic examination is crucial in the Maplewood case, where the lack of clear evidence has left detectives with few leads to follow.

One of the key components of profiling is understanding the psychological motivations behind criminal actions. Profilers often classify offenders into categories, such as organized or disorganized criminals, based on their behavior and the crime scene dynamics. Such classifications help detectives to anticipate the actions of suspects and strategize their approach during interviews. In Maplewood, knowing whether the suspect exhibits signs of organization or chaos can significantly impact the direction of the investigation.

Moreover, the role of forensic science cannot be overstated in the profiling process. Advances in technology have enabled investigators to analyze evidence with unprecedented precision. Forensic psychologists can assess behavioral patterns that emerge from the crime scene, offering insights that connect the dots between different cases. In the Maplewood mystery, forensic evidence intertwined with psychological profiling could lead to a breakthrough that has remained elusive for years.

Ultimately, profiling techniques serve as a bridge between the past and the present in cold cases. They allow detectives to revisit old cases with fresh eyes, applying modern understanding to long-standing mysteries. In Maplewood, these techniques not only provide a pathway to solving the case but also emphasize the necessity of persistence and patience in the pursuit of justice. As detectives delve deeper into the psychological aspects of the case, they bring renewed hope to a community yearning for closure.

The Impact of Motivation

Motivation plays a pivotal role in the world of detective fiction, particularly in stories that delve into unresolved mysteries like those found in "The Unsolved Case of Maplewood." For the investigator, motivation fuels persistence, guiding them through the labyrinthine paths of clues and testimonies. In the quiet town of Maplewood, where every face hides a story, the detective's determination to uncover the truth reflects the innate human drive to seek justice and closure. This motivation is not simply a plot device; it embodies the essence of what compels characters to act and react in the face of adversity.

The impact of motivation extends beyond the detective's personal journey. It influences how witnesses and suspects interact within the narrative. Each character's motivation reveals their intentions, whether it be fear of repercussions, the desire for redemption, or the need for truth. As the detective weaves through interviews, understanding these motivations becomes critical in piecing together the events surrounding the cold case. The complexity of human emotion and ambition adds a rich layer to the investigation, making the pursuit of truth a multifaceted endeavor.

Moreover, the theme of motivation raises intriguing questions about moral dilemmas faced by characters. In Maplewood, where secrets linger like the morning fog, the detective encounters individuals driven by conflicting desires. Some may wish to protect their loved ones, while others are consumed by guilt. This interplay of motivations not only propels the plot forward but also reflects the often gray nature of morality, urging readers to ponder the ethical implications of each character's choices. The detective's journey is not just about solving a case; it's about navigating the turbulent waters of human motivation.

The psychological profiling of characters based on their motivations further enriches the narrative. Understanding what drives individuals allows the detective to anticipate their actions and reactions, creating a more engaging and suspenseful story. For readers, this adds an element of depth to the traditional mystery format, transforming the investigation into a psychological exploration of the human condition. Each revelation about a character's motivation can shift the reader's perception, reinforcing the notion that nothing is as it seems in Maplewood.

In conclusion, motivation is a cornerstone of the investigative process in "The Unsolved Case of Maplewood." It shapes the narrative structure, drives character development, and enriches the reader's experience. The detective's unwavering quest for the truth is fueled by a complex web of motivations that intertwine the lives of all involved. As the story unfolds, it becomes clear that understanding these motivations is essential not only for solving the case but also for uncovering the deeper truths about the characters themselves and the secrets they hold.

Chapter 6: Legal Challenges

The Burden of Proof

In the intricate framework of detective fiction, the concept of the burden of proof plays a pivotal role. It is the responsibility of the investigator to gather sufficient evidence that not only suggests a suspect's guilt but also withstands scrutiny in the face of legal challenges. This principle is essential in the portrayal of classic detectives who rely on meticulous methods and unwavering persistence to unravel complex cases. The burden of proof is not merely a legal standard; it is a narrative device that drives the plot and deepens the reader's engagement with the unfolding mystery.

Taking the case of Maplewood, we find that the burden of proof presents a unique challenge for our detective. The town, steeped in secrets and whispers, holds clues that are often obscured by time and the memories of its residents. Each interview reveals fragments of truth, yet the investigator must discern which pieces of information are credible and which are fabrications born from fear or loyalty. This process reflects the painstaking work of real detectives who often navigate a labyrinth of human emotion and historical context to uncover the facts.

Forensic science emerges as a crucial ally in this endeavor. In the absence of eyewitness accounts or concrete testimony, forensic evidence provides the backbone of the investigation. Whether it's analyzing fibers found at the scene or examining old photographs for clues, the integration of science into the narrative elevates the story from mere speculation to a grounded pursuit of justice. Readers who appreciate methodical case-solving will find gratification in the way these elements interplay, creating a tapestry of evidence that ultimately leads to resolution.

Legal troubles also complicate the burden of proof in Maplewood's case. As the detective delves deeper, the implications of what is uncovered can have far-reaching consequences, not just for the suspects but for the community as a whole. The narrative tension builds as the reader is invited to ponder the ethical dilemmas faced by the investigator. Is it better to reveal the truth, even if it shatters lives, or to protect the community from the fallout? These moral quandaries resonate with fans of traditional mysteries who relish the psychological depth of their favorite stories.

Ultimately, the burden of proof is not just about establishing guilt or innocence; it is about the quest for truth in a world where certainty is often elusive. In "The Unsolved Case of Maplewood," this theme serves as a reminder that while the search for justice can be fraught with obstacles, the diligent pursuit of evidence and the unyielding spirit of inquiry are what define a true detective. As the story unfolds, readers are left contemplating their own beliefs about justice, truth, and the shadows that linger in small-town mysteries.

Courtroom Drama

The courtroom buzzed with anticipation as the trial of the century unfolded, drawing in spectators and journalists alike. The air was thick with tension as the defense attorney paced before the jury, his voice steady and confident, weaving a narrative that sought to unravel the very fabric of the prosecution's case. Each word was deliberate, designed to plant seeds of doubt in the minds of those tasked with delivering justice in the small town of Maplewood, where secrets ran deep and trust was a rare commodity.

As the trial progressed, the prosecution presented a meticulously constructed timeline, supported by forensic evidence that painted a chilling picture of the events leading to the crime. Witnesses took the stand, their testimonies laced with emotion, each recounting their version of the truth. The detective who had tirelessly pursued the case for years found himself on the witness list, his insights into the investigation shedding light on the complexities of the evidence and the psychological profiles of potential suspects.

With each passing day, the courtroom transformed into a theater of human drama, showcasing the frailty of memory and the intricacies of human behavior. The defense exploited every misstep, every inconsistency, to dismantle the prosecution's case brick by brick. It was a game of chess, where every move could mean the difference between freedom and incarceration, and the stakes had never been higher for the accused, whose fate hung in the balance.

The jury, composed of Maplewood's own residents, bore the weight of their decision with palpable gravitas. They were not just arbiters of guilt or innocence; they were witnesses to the unraveling of their community's fabric. As deliberations began, the tension in the courtroom was suffocating, each juror grappling with the moral ramifications of their verdict. The case had become more than just a trial; it was a reflection of the town's unresolved conflicts and the haunting specters of its past.

In the end, the verdict echoed through the hallowed halls, a culmination of months of painstaking investigation and courtroom drama. Yet, as the gavel fell, it became clear that for Maplewood, the case would never truly be closed. The unanswered questions lingered, like ghosts in the shadows, reminding everyone that in the pursuit of justice, some mysteries refuse to be solved, leaving behind a trail of doubt and speculation that would haunt the community for generations to come.

The Role of the Prosecutor

In the investigation of any crime, the prosecutor plays a pivotal role that often extends beyond the courtroom. They are not merely advocates for the state; they are also guardians of justice, ensuring that the rights of victims and the accused are balanced. In the case of Maplewood, the prosecutor's office was tasked with navigating a complex web of evidence and witness testimonies that had accumulated over the years. Their responsibility was to sift through this information meticulously, piecing together a narrative that would stand up in court while respecting the integrity of the ongoing investigation.

The prosecutor's approach to cold cases like the one in Maplewood is often characterized by perseverance and a deep understanding of forensic science. They collaborate closely with detectives and forensic experts, relying on the latest technologies and methodologies to re-examine old evidence. This partnership is crucial, as it allows them to utilize advancements in DNA analysis and other forensic techniques that may not have been available during the original investigation. Their ability to adapt and incorporate these new findings can often breathe new life into cases that have long since gone cold.

Moreover, the psychological profiling of potential suspects is another tool in the prosecutor's arsenal. Understanding the mindset and behaviors of criminals can provide invaluable insights into their motives and potential actions. In Maplewood, the prosecutor engaged with behavioral analysts to construct profiles that could lead to identifying the perpetrator. This method not only aids in narrowing down suspects but also informs the prosecution's strategy when presenting the case to a jury.

Legal troubles often arise in unsolved cases, presenting challenges that a prosecutor must navigate with skill and caution. There may be issues surrounding evidence admissibility, witness credibility, or even the potential for wrongful accusations. The prosecutor in Maplewood was acutely aware of these pitfalls, working diligently to ensure that every legal requirement was met while pursuing justice for the victims. Their commitment to upholding the law while seeking the truth exemplifies the delicate balance they must maintain throughout the legal process.

Ultimately, the role of the prosecutor in the investigation of the Maplewood case is one of unwavering determination and ethical responsibility. They are not only tasked with achieving a conviction but also with fostering public trust in the justice system.

As the case continues to unfold, the prosecutor's methods and decisions will be scrutinized, highlighting the complexities and pressures inherent in bringing long-standing mysteries to resolution. Their journey through the intricacies of this cold case reflects the profound impact that dedicated prosecutors have on the pursuit of justice in our communities.

Chapter 7: Secrets of Maplewood

The Town's Hidden Histories

Beneath the charming facade of Maplewood lies a tapestry of hidden histories waiting to be unraveled. The town, known for its picturesque streets and friendly faces, has its share of secrets that linger in the shadows. Old buildings, often overlooked, whisper tales of unresolved mysteries, each brick a testament to the lives lived and lost within their walls. The allure of these forgotten narratives draws in the curious, promising clues that may lead to answers long sought after but never found.

Every town has its legends, and Maplewood is no exception. The stories of the past are often interwoven with the present, creating an intricate web of connections that only the most dedicated of investigators can untangle. Local lore speaks of a series of disappearances that haunted the town decades ago, incidents that many would prefer to forget. Yet, for those willing to dig deeper, these chilling accounts serve as a gateway to understanding the complexities of the human psyche and the motivations behind such dark deeds.

Interviews with long-time residents reveal a collective memory that is both vivid and fragmented. Some recall the days when the police force was inundated with calls about strange occurrences, while others remember the palpable tension that gripped the community during the height of the investigations. The passage of time has not dulled these memories; rather, they have morphed into a shared narrative that unites the townspeople, binding them through a common history that is both tragic and intriguing.

Forensic science plays a pivotal role in piecing together these hidden histories. Advances in technology have opened new doors, allowing cold cases to be revisited with fresh eyes and innovative methods. As detectives sift through old evidence, they are often met with unexpected breakthroughs that challenge previous assumptions. These scientific revelations not only shed light on the mysteries of the past but also provide a renewed sense of purpose for those dedicated to solving what may seem unsolvable.

Ultimately, the quest to uncover Maplewood's hidden histories is not just about solving a mystery; it's about understanding the human condition. The stories of those who lived, loved, and lost in this small town reflect broader themes of resilience, betrayal, and redemption. As the investigation unfolds, it becomes clear that the past is never truly buried—it lingers, waiting for someone brave enough to bring it back to the surface and confront the truths that have long been obscured.

Suspects and Alibis

In the small town of Maplewood, the investigation into the mysterious disappearance of local resident, Edward Hargrove, has led detectives down a labyrinth of suspects and alibis. The townsfolk, tightly knit and often wary of outsiders, present a complex web of relationships. Each person connected to Edward seems to hold a piece of the puzzle, yet the truth remains obscured behind their conflicting stories. As detectives sift through the interviews, the challenge is not only to establish who was where on that fateful night but also to understand the motives that might have driven them to conceal the truth.

Among the primary suspects is Hargrove's business partner, Martin Lee, who has a history of financial troubles. Martin claims he was at a charity gala miles away when Edward disappeared, but a lack of corroborating witnesses raises suspicions. His alibi, while seemingly solid, begins to show cracks under scrutiny. Detectives revisit the scene of the gala, interviewing attendees who might have seen Martin, hoping to either confirm his whereabouts or unravel a more sinister connection to the case.

Then there is Sarah Jenkins, Edward's estranged sister, who returned to Maplewood just days before the incident. Her reasons for coming home are shrouded in mystery, and her alibi seems almost too convenient. She insists she was visiting a friend that evening, but the friend's own timeline fails to align perfectly. The detectives recognize the psychological dynamics at play; family secrets often breed deep-seated resentments, and it's not uncommon for those closest to a victim to harbor the darkest motives.

As the investigation progresses, the detectives rely heavily on forensic science to validate or invalidate these alibis. Evidence collected from Edward's home, including fingerprints and digital footprints, provides crucial insights into who may have been there leading up to his disappearance. Each piece of evidence is meticulously analyzed in the lab, revealing a timeline that may contradict the suspects' claims, ultimately leading them closer to the truth.

Ultimately, the case of Edward Hargrove challenges the detectives to remain persistent and methodical, as small-town mysteries often hide the most significant secrets. The layers of deception require patience and skill to uncover. With each interview and piece of evidence, they inch closer to unraveling the tangled web of suspects and alibis, determined to bring closure to a case that has haunted Maplewood for far too long.

Gossip and Rumors

In the small town of Maplewood, gossip and rumors weave a tapestry that often obscures the truth. Each whispered word carries weight, echoing through the close-knit community and affecting lives in profound ways. When Detective Samuel Hayes began his investigation into the unsolved case, he quickly learned that the local populace had strong opinions and speculations about the crime, and these narratives were not always grounded in reality. It became clear that the stories circulating could either help or hinder his pursuit of the truth.

The roots of gossip in Maplewood ran deep, often tracing back to the town's historical events and long-held grudges. Residents held onto memories like heirlooms, passing them down through generations, shaping perceptions of one another. As Hayes interviewed townsfolk, he encountered conflicting accounts that painted a murky picture of the events surrounding the case. Some claimed to know the perpetrator, while others pointed fingers at the innocent, illustrating how fear and suspicion can distort facts.

Each conversation revealed layers of complexity within the community, where alliances were formed and broken based on the latest rumors. Hayes noted how easily a simple piece of information could spiral into a full-blown scandal. It was not uncommon for a casual remark to snowball into accusations that could tarnish reputations overnight. This phenomenon was particularly evident in Maplewood, where the stakes were high, and the desire to protect loved ones often overshadowed the need for honesty.

As the investigation progressed, Hayes found himself sifting through the debris of these rumors, trying to separate fact from fiction. He realized that while gossip could lead to valuable insights, it was often misleading. The detective had to rely on his training and instincts, conducting thorough interviews and meticulously examining evidence to find clarity amid the chaos. Each piece of information had to be verified, and every source scrutinized, illustrating the challenges faced by those who pursue justice in a world filled with half-truths.

Ultimately, the interplay of gossip and rumors in Maplewood served as both a hindrance and a guide for Hayes. It highlighted the human condition—our tendency to speculate and judge based on limited information. In a town where everyone knew everyone, the quest for truth became even more complicated. Yet, through perseverance and a commitment to uncovering reality, Hayes remained determined to solve the case that had haunted Maplewood for far too long, proving that even in a world rife with speculation, the truth could still emerge from the shadows.

Chapter 8: Renewed Hope

A Fresh Perspective

In the quaint town of Maplewood, where every corner seems to whisper secrets of the past, a fresh perspective on an unsolved mystery can breathe life into dormant clues. Detective Sarah Lawson, known for her methodical approach and unyielding determination, returns to the case of the vanished schoolteacher, a case that has haunted the community for decades. With a new set of eyes and modern forensic techniques at her disposal, she embarks on a journey that will challenge the very foundations of the investigation.

As Sarah delves deeper, she uncovers layers of complexity that had been overlooked. Old interviews with witnesses, once deemed inconsequential, now hold the key to understanding the relationships and dynamics of the town's residents. The echoes of their testimonies, coupled with advancements in psychological profiling, reveal the hidden motives that may have driven someone to silence a beloved figure. Each piece of evidence brings her closer to unraveling the truth.

The community's reluctance to revisit the tragedy reflects a broader theme of unresolved grief. Many residents harbor their own theories, each more elaborate than the last, but all lacking the rigor of a proper investigation. Sarah's fresh perspective not only seeks to solve the mystery but also aims to heal the wounds that have festered in the hearts of those left behind. Her approach is not just about finding answers; it's about restoring faith in the institution of justice.

Utilizing forensic science, Sarah re-examines the physical evidence collected from the scene, applying new techniques that were unavailable during the initial investigations. DNA analysis, digital footprints, and advanced crime scene reconstruction become essential tools in her quest. The application of these modern methods is a stark reminder that time may obscure the truth, but it can also illuminate it. Each discovery is a step toward closure, not just for the case but for the entire town.

In Maplewood, the ghosts of the past linger, but with Sarah's relentless pursuit of the truth, there is hope for resolution. As she pieces together the fragments of a life interrupted, her fresh perspective transforms the narrative from one of despair to one of possibility. This case, once a closed chapter, now promises to reveal deeper truths about the human condition, the resilience of a community, and the enduring quest for justice.

New Witnesses Come Forward

As the investigation into the Maplewood case trudged on, a surprising turn of events unfolded. New witnesses, previously silent, began to step forward, each with their own fragment of the puzzle that had eluded detectives for years. They came from different walks of life, yet their stories intertwined in ways that suggested a deeper connection to the unsolved mystery. Their testimonies, however, were not without contradictions, leaving detectives to sift through the haze of uncertainty that had clouded the case for so long.

Among the new witnesses was an elderly man who claimed to have seen a suspicious vehicle parked near the crime scene on the night of the incident. His memory, although faded, sparked a glimmer of hope for the detectives, who meticulously documented every detail he provided. Interviews with him revealed a wealth of information about the small town's dynamics and its inhabitants, shedding light on relationships that had long been buried beneath secrets and gossip. However, the challenge lay in verifying his account against the existing evidence.

Another witness, a woman who had recently moved back to Maplewood after years away, recounted a chilling encounter with a figure she believed to be connected to the case. Her vivid description of a man lurking near her childhood home during the investigation resonated with detectives, prompting them to re-examine old leads. This unforeseen development reignited the team's determination, pushing them to delve deeper into the past and explore connections that had previously gone unnoticed.

As the detectives began to connect the dots, they encountered the complex web of human emotions and memories that often accompany unresolved cases. Each new testimony came with layers of fear, regret, and the desire for closure. The detectives had to navigate not only the facts presented but also the psychological intricacies of the witnesses, understanding that their motivations could impact the reliability of their accounts. This required a delicate balance of empathy and skepticism as they worked to build a clearer picture of the events that transpired.

With each new witness, the momentum of the investigation shifted, revealing that the case was still alive and breathing. The detectives knew that the more they uncovered, the closer they were to solving a mystery that had haunted Maplewood for decades. As they pieced together the narratives of the witnesses, the potential for resolution became palpable, and the once-dormant case began to pulse with renewed energy, reminding everyone involved that sometimes, the past has a way of resurfacing when we least expect it.

The Turning Point

The morning air was thick with anticipation as Detective Jameson stood at the edge of Maplewood, a small town cloaked in secrets. It had been years since the unsolved case of Sarah Mitchell had haunted him, the echoes of her disappearance still resonating in the quiet streets. Today, however, felt different; the weight of unresolved questions pressed heavily on his chest, urging him to take a step forward into the heart of the mystery. The turning point had arrived, and it was time to unravel the threads that had long been tangled.

Jameson revisited the evidence that had been meticulously gathered over the years, each piece a fragment of a larger puzzle. He could almost hear the whispers of the townsfolk as he combed through the file, their opinions and suspicions swirling around him like autumn leaves. The interviews conducted years ago had yielded little, but perhaps a fresh perspective would shine a light on the shadows that clouded the truth. With renewed determination, he reached out to those who had once shared their thoughts, hoping to unearth new clues that might point him in the right direction.

As he re-engaged with the community, Jameson felt the walls of silence beginning to crack. The townspeople, once hesitant to speak, seemed to sense his unwavering commitment to finding answers. One by one, they shared their memories, some tinged with regret, others laced with fear of retribution. Each conversation was a step closer to the truth, revealing connections and patterns that had eluded him before. The turning point was not just in the evidence, but in the willingness of the community to confront their past.

The pivotal moment came when an elderly resident, Mrs. Thompson, recalled a seemingly trivial detail from the day Sarah vanished. It was an offhand remark about a stranger seen lingering near the local diner, a detail that had been overlooked in previous investigations. Jameson felt a rush of adrenaline; this was the breakthrough he had been waiting for. With a new lead in hand, he began to delve into the lives of those who frequented the diner, uncovering a web of relationships that intertwined with Sarah's life.

With each discovery, the case transformed from a cold relic of the past to a living, breathing investigation. Jameson realized that the turning point was not merely a singular event but a series of moments fueled by persistence and the courage to confront uncomfortable truths. As he pieced together the evidence and followed the leads, the fog of uncertainty began to lift, revealing the path toward justice for Sarah Mitchell. The case that had refused to close was finally on the brink of resolution, and Jameson was determined to see it through to the end.

Chapter 9: The Chase for Truth

Following New Leads

In the world of cold cases, the pursuit of new leads is both an art and a science. Detectives often find themselves revisiting old files, scrutinizing every detail with fresh eyes. Each piece of evidence has the potential to unlock a new avenue of investigation, making persistence key in the quest for the truth. The challenge lies not only in uncovering new information but also in piecing it together effectively. The thrill of a potential breakthrough can reignite the passion of even the most seasoned investigator.

Interviews with witnesses or informants often yield surprising results. Over time, memories can shift, and new perspectives may emerge, allowing detectives to gather previously overlooked details. In small towns like Maplewood, the interconnectedness of the community can lead to unexpected revelations. A casual conversation may unearth a forgotten clue, or a local might finally feel ready to share what they know. This human element is crucial in following new leads, as personal connections can often bridge the gap between suspicion and clarity.

Forensic science plays a significant role in re-examining cold cases. Advances in technology have transformed the way evidence is analyzed, allowing for new methods to uncover the truth. Techniques such as DNA analysis and digital forensics provide a wealth of opportunities for detectives. In the case of Maplewood, revisiting physical evidence with state-of-the-art methods could reveal links to suspects long gone from memory. This intersection of old-fashioned detective work and modern science creates a powerful tool in solving lingering mysteries.

The psychological profiling of criminals also becomes vital when following new leads. Understanding the mindset and motives behind a crime can guide detectives in their investigation. By analyzing patterns and behaviors, investigators can better predict where to look for new evidence or whom to interview next. The complexity of human behaviors in small-town settings adds layers to the investigation, as personal relationships often complicate the narrative surrounding a crime.

Ultimately, the journey of following new leads is filled with challenges and rewards. The process can be slow and frustrating, but the potential for resolution drives detectives forward. Each new piece of information brings them closer to closure, not only for themselves but also for the families affected by the unresolved case. In Maplewood, the case may have refused to close, but with each new lead, a glimmer of hope remains that the truth will eventually surface, bringing light to the shadows that have lingered for too long.

A Race Against Time

In the quiet town of Maplewood, time seemed to stand still, especially when it came to the unsolved mysteries that haunted its streets. Detective Samuel Graves, a seasoned investigator with a keen eye for detail, found himself drawn into a case that had eluded resolution for over a decade. As he reviewed the evidence, he felt the weight of the years pressing upon him, fueling a sense of urgency. Each tick of the clock echoed the frustration of families still seeking answers, and Graves knew he had to act swiftly before the trail grew colder.

The investigation began with a series of interviews, each recounting the fateful events surrounding the disappearance of young Emily Harris. As Graves meticulously questioned witnesses, he uncovered discrepancies in their stories that hinted at deeper secrets lurking beneath the surface. He noted the subtle shifts in body language and the fleeting glances exchanged between the townsfolk, suggesting that the truth was not as straightforward as it seemed. With each conversation, he pieced together a puzzle that had long been neglected, but time was not on his side.

Graves turned to forensic science to breathe life into the faded evidence, revisiting the crime scene with a fresh perspective. Utilizing advanced techniques, he hoped to extract new information from old clues. The scent of damp earth and the chill in the air reminded him of the urgency of his task. It was during this process that he discovered a critical piece of evidence—a forgotten item that could change everything. The race against time intensified, as he realized that the longer the truth remained buried, the more likely it would slip away forever.

As the investigation unfolded, the psychological profiling of potential suspects became pivotal. Graves delved into the minds of those who had been close to Emily, exploring their motivations and possible connections to the case. It was a delicate dance, trying to discern the truth from the webs of lies. Each profile painted a picture of desperation and fear, revealing the lengths to which individuals might go to protect their secrets. The closer he got to the truth, the more dangerous the stakes became.

With the clock ticking down, Graves faced mounting pressure from both the community and his superiors. The unresolved case loomed large, threatening to define his career. Yet, he remained steadfast in his pursuit of justice for Emily. As he connected the dots, he realized that the answers lay not just in the evidence, but in the very heart of Maplewood itself. The town's secrets, entwined with its history, were waiting to be uncovered, and Graves was determined to unearth them before it was too late.

The Final Confrontation

The night was thick with anticipation as Detective Mark Reynolds prepared for the final confrontation. The small town of Maplewood, known for its quiet streets and friendly faces, was about to reveal its darkest secrets. Reynolds had spent years piecing together the fragments of a cold case that had haunted him since he first stepped into the precinct. With each clue, each interview, he was drawn deeper into a web of deception that had woven itself through the fabric of the community. Tonight, everything would come to a head.

As he approached the old Maplewood Mill, the site where the last evidence had been found, the weight of unresolved questions pressed heavily on his shoulders. This was not just a case of solving a murder; it was about uncovering the truth that had eluded so many before him. The chilling wind whispered through the trees, almost as if it were urging him forward. He recalled the faces of the witnesses who had shared their stories, the pain in their eyes as they spoke of loss. Each interview had been a step closer to the truth, but this was the moment of reckoning.

Inside the mill, shadows danced on the walls, and the air was thick with tension. Reynolds's heart raced as he prepared to confront the suspect who had evaded justice for far too long. The man had lived with his secrets, hiding in plain sight among the townsfolk, who trusted him. Reynolds had gathered enough evidence to warrant this confrontation, but he knew that the real challenge lay in breaking down the walls that the suspect had built around himself. It was time to peel back the layers of lies.

As he stepped into the dimly lit room, their eyes met, and a silence fell between them, heavy with unspoken words. Reynolds took a deep breath, recalling the meticulous notes he had kept over the years. He would not let this moment slip away. With each question he posed, he could see the suspect's composure beginning to crack. The truth was like a tightly wound spring, ready to explode at any moment. Every detail, every piece of evidence, was a thread in the tapestry of this case, and Reynolds was determined to unravel it.

In the end, the confrontation was not just about the resolution of a murder; it was about the healing of a community. As the suspect finally admitted to the crime, the weight of the years began to lift from Reynolds's shoulders. The case that had refused to close was now on the brink of resolution. Maplewood would never be the same, but perhaps, with the truth finally out, the town could begin to heal the scars of its past. The final confrontation had not only brought an end to a long pursuit of justice but had also restored a sense of peace to a town shrouded in mystery and fear.

Chapter 10: The Case That Refused to Close

Reflections on the Journey

As I reflect on the journey through the unsolved case of Maplewood, a peculiar sense of nostalgia washes over me. Each twist and turn in the investigation has not only shaped the narrative but also left an indelible mark on those who live in the shadows of this small town. The relentless pursuit of truth has drawn many, from seasoned detectives to amateur sleuths, each contributing to the rich tapestry of theories and insights that surround this perplexing mystery.

The methodical approach taken during the investigation often felt like walking a tightrope, balancing the weight of evidence with the fragility of human emotions. Interviews conducted in dimly lit rooms, the scent of stale coffee hanging in the air, revealed more than just facts; they unearthed the fears and hopes of a community yearning for closure. It is this intricate dance of clues and confessions that highlights the essence of detective work, where every detail holds the potential to shift the narrative in unexpected ways.

Cold case investigations, such as this one, showcase the importance of persistence over time. The passage of years can sometimes blur the lines between memory and reality, yet they also provide the clarity needed to sift through the debris of forgotten lives. Each revisit to the scene, each new witness, and every piece of evidence collected serves as a testament to the unwavering dedication of those who refuse to let the case fade into obscurity.

In grappling with the psychological profiles of the individuals involved, we uncover layers of complexity that challenge our preconceived notions of right and wrong. Understanding the motivations and fears of both the victims and suspects transforms the investigation from a simple whodunit into a profound exploration of the human condition. It is this psychological depth that captivates readers and invites them to immerse themselves in the unfolding drama of Maplewood.

Ultimately, the journey through the unsolved case of Maplewood is more than just a search for answers; it is a reflection of the human spirit's resilience. Each clue, each interview, and each theory crafted over the years speaks to our innate desire for resolution. As we continue to unravel the layers of this mystery, we not only seek justice for those who have been wronged but also find a deeper understanding of ourselves and the world around us.

The Impact on the Community

The unresolved case of Maplewood has cast a long shadow over the community, stirring a whirlwind of emotions among its residents. For years, whispers of the mystery have lingered in the air, fueling speculation and curiosity. The tragic events that unfolded not only impacted the victims' families but also created a palpable tension among neighbors who once shared close ties. As the investigation dragged on, the community found itself divided, with some advocating for closure while others were hesitant to confront the past.

Local businesses, once bustling with life, began to feel the strain of the case's notoriety. Tourists who once flocked to Maplewood for its charm now hesitated, wary of the dark tale that surrounded the town. The fear of being associated with an unsolved crime loomed large, as shop owners struggled to maintain their livelihood amidst the mounting unease. This economic ripple effect highlighted how deeply intertwined the community's identity was with the unresolved case, revealing an unsettling truth about the costs of lingering mystery.

The emotional toll on residents became evident during town meetings, where discussions about the case often turned heated. Longtime friends found themselves on opposing sides, with some seeking justice for the victims and others preferring to let bygones be bygones. This rift not only affected relationships but also instilled a sense of distrust, as secrets and suspicions festered in the silence. The case, intended to bring the community together in pursuit of truth, instead became a source of division, complicating the already sensitive atmosphere.

As the years passed, the case's impact extended beyond the immediate community. Investigators and journalists from outside Maplewood began to take an interest, shining a spotlight on the town. This external attention brought new hope for resolution but also intensified the scrutiny of the residents' lives. Those who had lived through the events found themselves grappling not only with their memories but also with the perceptions of outsiders, forcing them to confront the reality of their situation in an entirely new light.

Ultimately, the unresolved case of Maplewood serves as a poignant reminder of how a single incident can reverberate through the fabric of a community. The legacy of the mystery continues to shape the lives of its inhabitants, leaving an indelible mark on their collective psyche. As residents navigate the complexities of their intertwined fates, they must confront the ghosts of the past and work towards healing, proving that the quest for truth and closure is a journey that transcends time and circumstance.

Lessons Learned for Future Investigations

In the investigation of the Maplewood case, several lessons emerged that could shape future inquiries into unsolved mysteries. One crucial takeaway is the importance of persistence. Investigators must remain dedicated to uncovering the truth, even when faced with obstacles or dead ends. This case illustrated that sometimes, the most vital clues are hidden beneath layers of time and neglect, waiting for someone to dig deep and bring them to light.

Another significant lesson learned is the value of community involvement in solving cases. The Maplewood investigation benefited immensely from the input of local residents who had insights or memories that could assist the detectives. Engaging the community can provide essential leads and foster a sense of cooperation that may motivate individuals to share information they might otherwise withhold.

Forensic science continues to evolve, and this case highlighted the necessity of keeping up with advancements in technology. Retesting evidence with modern techniques can yield new revelations that were previously unattainable. Investigators should prioritize revisiting older cases with fresh eyes and updated methods, as this could mean the difference between resolution and continued mystery.

Psychological profiling also played a role in understanding the potential motives behind the crime. Understanding the mindset of suspects can inform investigative strategies and lead to more focused questioning. Future cases may benefit from a more integrated approach that combines traditional detective work with psychological insights, enhancing the likelihood of uncovering the truth.

Lastly, legal complexities often surround cold cases, complicating investigations. The Maplewood case underscored the importance of navigating these legal hurdles with care. Investigators must be well-versed in legal frameworks to ensure that their pursuit of justice does not inadvertently infringe upon rights or procedural guidelines. Learning to balance investigative zeal with legal prudence is vital for the success of future inquiries. It's a beautiful day

Author Richard Trillion Mantey

Author Biography

Richard Trillion Mantey is an author, thinker, and storyteller dedicated to crafting narratives that go beyond entertainment—stories that explore the deeper layers of human experience, psychology, and truth.

Known for his powerful voice and insightful perspective, Richard writes with a rare balance of emotional depth and intellectual clarity. His work often bridges the gap between suspense and reflection, inviting readers not only to follow a story—but to feel it, question it, and grow from it.

With a passion for understanding how people think, act, and respond under pressure, Richard brings a compelling authenticity to his writing. His storytelling is shaped by a deep curiosity about human behavior, the pursuit of truth, and the unseen forces that influence decisions and outcomes.

In The Unsolved Case of Maplewood, he combines suspenseful narrative with real-world themes—exploring forensic science, criminal psychology, and the emotional weight carried by unresolved events.

Richard's mission is simple yet powerful:

To write stories that stay with you long after the final page.